To Whom It May Concern

To Whom It May Concern

by
Bob MacKenzie

Dark Matter Press
Kingston, Canada

First published
as an e-book
2006
by Amazon Shorts

Library and Archives Canada Cataloguing in Publication

MacKenzie, Bob, 1947-
To whom it may concern / by Bob Mackenzie.

ISBN 978-0-9685422-3-1

I. Title.

PS8575.K424T6 2010   C813'.54   C2010-906096-2

To a young girl I met so long ago
who had a beautiful black crow
and a captivating sense of magic.

For in and out, above, about, below,
Tis nothing but a Magic Shadow-show,
Play'd in a Box whose Candle is the Sun,
Round which we Phantom Figures come and go.

Rubáiyát of Omar Khayyám
tr. Edward Fitzgerald

To Whom It May Concern

The room is empty. It is the kitchen cum dining area of a low rental upstairs apartment near the centre of the city. There is a small, sparsely furnished living room through the archway to the east, a bedroom north of that and a bathroom south of the kitchen. Like the rest of the apartment, this room is spartan in appearance, very clean, furnished only with the bare necessities: second-hand curtains on the westward facing windows above the kitchen sink and on the small window in the door, an old rounded faced refrigerator in the south-west corner next to the bathroom door, an equally old gas stove slotted in between the fridge and the counter which runs along the rest of that wall and contains the ceramic sink; in the centre of the room, under a cracked sun-shaped fixture, an old wooden dining table, small, possibly oak, and four mismatched wooden chairs around it. On closer examination it can be seen that the eastward edge of the table and parts of the westward facing chair show minimal but nevertheless obvious scorch marks, as though they had been through a fire at some time. On the floor beside the chair several pieces of letter paper are strewn, almost carelessly, almost as though a letter had been written, or read, and then dropped.

The girl: I have been here before. Not this room, perhaps, but this circumstance. When he was eight I met him at dusk; I impressed him with my crow, trained to perch on my wrist or shoulder, trained to obey my every command. In the growing darkness I worried him with my black bird. A twelve year old girl who seems to control nature was beyond his understanding. I lit a cigarette and, while smoking, flipped it with my tongue backward into my mouth; seeing he was impressed, I held it, only a small round circle showing through my lips, and smoked it from inside my mouth. I lit a candle and passed my hand through the flame, a simple trick any human can do. I held my hand in the flame. He was awed. It began to rain and the flame flickered bluish. I allowed the flame to assume my hand, assume my arm, assume myself, and I was gone home.

The man: The window was easy, an easily slid sash and a rush of wind, and I was in. The child was asleep. I walked quietly to the crib; it was like a cage. I felt sad for the poor imprisoned soul. I thought the child was asleep. I rose above him to see better. He awoke. I beckoned to see if he would come; he cried. An error—the blue! the blue, the blue...

"Sir, ah, Sergeant Cooper, I think I've found something: a sort of a letter, looks like he might have written it."

"A letter? To who Jack?"

"Nobody. That is, it's addressed 'to whom it may concern;' it was just laying on the floor here, and, ah..."

"Yes? What is it?"

"Well, sir, some of the edges are burnt, almost like someone tried to destroy it and the fire didn't take, you know."

"So what's it say? Is there anything that will help us to figure out what's been going on here?"

"Maybe, let me look at..."

To Whom It May Concern:

I suppose I have known since childhood that I must someday write this letter, yet it seems very unreal now that the moment is here. I am writing, I guess, to try and explain, although I am not sure exactly how I can, what is happening. I don't think any of the others ever knew. If they did, they never told. And if anyone else knew, or saw, they too kept it a secret. Maybe they tried, the others like me; I know it is difficult, even in normal circumstances, to explain. Now, in the heat of this moment, as I feel mind, body racing faster and faster, I wonder how coherent I can be, stay.

There is a cycle; of that I am certain. I don't know exactly how it works. It's something that no one talks about. I have tried to trace other families. Information is hard to get—they prefer to forget—but it seems to come to every third or fourth generation in most cases. Maybe that is why I know ahead and others don't; we seem to be the exception to the rule, have one every generation. Alternate: male, female, male, female. Always the first child: me! My mother, grandfather, great grandmother, on back, always the female side of the family. And no one talks about it, not until it's old enough to be myth, three generations or more sometimes.

I learned by mistake. Heard my aunt and mother, sisters, talking about their grandmother, sitting at peace on the verandah, rocking and knitting I think they said. And lightning, or something, and her gone; on the prairies sudden cloudbursts and sudden lightning, what they call heat lightning, are not unknown. She burned, they said, burned in a sudden electric flash of blue. They too had only heard the story by accident, she being gone before they were born. My grandfather died one autumn while working in the fields. The consensus was lightning; a storm had been in the offing. The wheat was scorched, not burned; only he was burned: completely! My mother was only about twelve or thirteen then, the same age I was when she died. They never told me about my mother. They never had to. My father said heart attack. I never saw the body.

There were the visitors. Almost since I was born I saw them. A man, terrifying, sliding in my window, me an infant in my crib, standing by me, looking, then floating in the air over me, a devil beckoning me. Why? I screamed. He vanished into a blue haze. I couldn't talk. I could not tell. When I could tell, not just this one but others that came after I could speak, no one believed me. My mother

4

looked like she knew, but always she denied my stories as fantasies. I stopped telling. A girl, dusk; I am walking down a country road on my way home. The road is a small one because there is grass down the middle, between the dirt tracks; on my right are open fields of swaying wheat and barley, some fallow fields too, on my left a poplar windbreak. She has a great black bird, a raven or crow or something, that seems to understand her, speak to her, obey. She smokes a cigarette; later, on a visit to the Philippines, I will see ancient women, lots of them, smoking like that, only the very tip showing, the burning spark somewhere deep in the throat. At the time it seems like magic. She lights a candle, slices the flame with her hand, holds her hand still, is engulfed in blue fire that climbs her arm, outlines her figure. She is gone. Noticing that it is raining, I walk home quickly in the blue haze of dusk.

It's getting faster, more confusing, the heat—the heat is getting unbearable; I must continue, explain what I am feeling. I feel like a foreseen car accident; my mind races so everything becomes slow motion, my hand crawling painstakingly across the page painstakingly slow as I write this, everything unreal like some movie I must have seen somewhere. The heat! It can't be! The landlord must have the heat too high. It can't, must not be me! I feel I am burning up; I am still writing though; I don't see it yet—the burning is only a feeling—I have so much more to

"That's it."

"That's it? It doesn't even make sense. He stopped in mid-sentence? Does that make sense to you, Jack?"

"No sir, sounds almost like he was high or crazy or something."

"Maybe."

"What did the neighbours say? Anything?"

"Not much. He was quiet. Didn't seem like a drunk or anything: no loud noises, apparently no television or radio, no friends calling—funny though..."

"Funny?"

"Mr. Garber, across the alley, he was surprised to see the TV—said he'd never seen it before that night..."

"How did he see the TV; was he here?

"No. No, he said he looked out around midnight, to check the weather or something. Said he never knew there was a TV here. You know how, sometimes, when a television set is on, you can see the blue light flashing and flickering through the curtains, and you know it's on...that's what he said he saw that night. In the kitchen, no less! The kitchen window faces Mr. Garber's."

"There is none."

"What? What's that supposed to mean, Jack? None, what?"

"TV set. I've been through every room. There is no television set. Nowhere."

"That could help explain things, if the TV was stolen. Is there a stereo?"

"No."

The girl: I saw him once. He was about twenty two, harried looking, obvious loner. I had a class act, used magic to enhance the dance: good sound, good lights, mellow music developing to a storm sequence; a class act! It was the Tanganyika Tavern. Men liked me; I looked about twelve or thirteen. My pet crow helped. He would do anything I said. Like I said, I saw him once, after I had stripped down, almost to my G-string, which was all that was allowed downtown. He asked to talk to me–after. Of course, I said no. It was the finale. The flashing blue lights came on. They intensified. I, as usual, vanished. He looked astounded; as though it was real.

The mother: He was always different, my Gilbert. We joked about it, said he was born a month later than due because he was stubborn; in fact, he was a couple of weeks late. He was clever, and a loner. Even as a baby he seemed aloof, never warm and cuddly like his younger sister, and as a young boy he never developed close friends. Even his young acquaintances were few. He seemed always to be alone, reading or walking in the countryside. His father and I never seemed able to reach him in terms of love, our love. Only logic appealed to him. He was clever, still is. Nothing can be said or done without him questioning, probing, proving, confirming facts for himself. Yet that is really why, now that he is approaching his twelfth birthday, he seems so strange. With all his cleverness and logic he seems to be living in a world of fantasy. He has an obsession with something he read, a sort of phenomenon called spontaneous human combustion. Apparently he saw it in some magazine, thinks that certain people throughout history have vanished instantly in a puff of blue flame. He seems to think that, because a couple of people in my family have been struck by lightning, not that abnormal a prairie occurrance, my family is subject to this phenomenon. And he thinks it is forecastable, in his fantasy imagines that I am next. I am worried about him. He has made up other stories, wierd stories. Could he be expressing some sort of suppressed anger at me? I wonder. Where could I have gone wrong? I can't even talk to him now. He avoids me. Acts as though I might go up in smoke right before his eyes. I have spoken with his father about this, and we have both talked to the doctor. None of us seems able to get beneath the surface, to discover the source of this fantasy. Now it seems all that is left for me to do is try and sort out my thoughts in this journal, write them down and see if I can find out where I went wrong, see if I can yet help my poor Gilbert.

"You suppose he just took off? You know, maybe too many debts or something?"

"Not likely, Jack. He seems to have paid for everything in cash, even the rent. That's why the landlord called us when he went missing for two weeks after failing to pay the rent. Besides, all his stuff is still here. Even his clothes!"

"Still, it seems weird. I mean, him vanishing like that into thin air, and not a sign of violence, not a sign of where he went–it's strange. Hey, if there were couple of half eaten meals in here this place could rank as a land-bound Marie Celeste."

"A what?"

"You know, that ship. A hundred and some years ago they found it at sea. All the sails were set but there was nobody on board, no signs of piracy or anything, meals half eaten, drinks half drunk, everybody vanished–very spooky!"

"You don't really believe in that stuff?"

"Maybe. I mean, there are lots of cases recorded where things happen that nobody can explain. And look here: the unfinished letter, and what about the TV, supposedly never here yet turned on, at least apparently turned on the last night he was here. Who knows, Sergeant Cooper, who knows...."

"Come on! Let's check around here once more to see if we can find anything else before we go."

Grade Six English Assignment: I am young. I am not yet one year old. I am dreaming. I cannot speak. I can understand, some. I am dreaming another place, another time. In my dream I am still a baby, but I have control over my space. I can move: through space, through time. I am in a room. It seems like an old room. Several doors and an archway lead off it. Thinking back now, it seems like a kitchen; there is a fridge, a stove, a sink, things like that, and a wooden table. There is a man at the table. He is busy writing something and does not see me. Maybe he can't see me. Maybe he is part of my dream without me being part of his. I move around the room, looking at everything. It is a very plain room. The man writes; I wonder what. I rise through the air. For some reason I am not surprised that I can do this. I move to a point directly above the table. Too far above, the words blur. I settle on my cushion of air: lower, lower, lower. I hope the man will not notice me. The words begin to be clear. This page, the one he is writing, is not the first. I look at the last few words:

> *She is gone.*
> *Noticing that it is raining, I walk home*
> *quickly in the blue haze of dusk.*
> *It's getting faster...*

He is still writing. I look to the finished sheets beside his other hand. The right, I think. He must be left handed, writing with his left. I start to read what appears to be the first page, "To Whom It May Concern"....

I stop reading. I sense someone else in the room. I see no one. Still. The room is still. The man stops writing. He looks around. He looks like he too has sensed someone, maybe me. No. He looks up. Looks right through me. I look behind me. No one. I look back at the man. There is a candle on the table. There was none before. He notices too, reaches toward it. As his left hand touches the candle the flame bends down as though driven by a sudden gust of wind, grows, welcomes and wraps his hand as hand and flame turn bright blue. He grabs his papers with his other hand, holds them out, away from the table, away from the flame. The blue rushes up his arm, outlines his figure. As his right arm is wrapped in fire he drops a flutter of white sheets to the floor. I see his mouth open, wide. He says something; there is anger. Then fear, he is screaming. I hear nothing, suddenly realize I can only see, not hear him. I am aware of a black shadow across the bright blue glow of the room. I hear a coarse sound, screech like a crow's cry in flight—no! like a scream, my scream. My mouth is open wide. I am screaming. I am home in my crib, screaming. My mother comes in, consoling, comforting, asking what is wrong, asking...I cannot speak.

Thomas Cooper, City Police Staff Sergeant: I really cannot comment on any case, even a closed missing persons, with any magazine, including yours, Mr. Harper. I'm sorry your editor has sent you on such a wild goose chase, but my answer must be, and is, no comment.

Jack Knight, City Police Constable: Okay, Mr. Harper, as long as you promise to keep my name out of it, I can use the money. There really wasn't much to pursue. That's why they dropped the missing persons case. There was no sign of violence, and the landlord wouldn't file a complaint about the rent. There was no family we could locate, so we had nowhere to go with an investigation. Here's all we know:

His name was Gilbert Duane Endrede, usually went by Gil. Born and raised in the prairies. Seems always to have been a loner, few male friends and even fewer female. Very clever in school. In grade six he wrote a story--supernatural stuff like you use in your magazine--that his teacher entered in a national competition. Honourable mention for that one. He grew up wanting to be a writer. Never seems to have written much, except for six months he worked at a weekly newspaper. Mostly worked odd jobs. Never seemed to make much of himself but always managed to pay his own way, cash. His mother died at thirty one. It seemed to hit him hard. If he was a loner before, he was even more of one after. Only one serious girl boy relationship. He got her pregnant then skipped. The mother kept the girl. She'd be about twelve now.

Hey, listen, I got a lot of detail on this, all written down; it's my own checking, don't say it's the police records, okay. I'm just interested in these things, disappearances and such, you know

I'll give you copies of what I have here. I've shown you copies of the report Sergeant Cooper and I wrote up, so you know pretty well everything, about the blue light, television or whatever, and the note, you have a copy there–it begins, "To Whom It May Concern"....

Christina had just turned twelve when she brought the crow home. Her mother let her keep it, perhaps in compensation for the child never having known a father.

Besides, it made her feel good to see her daughter totally involved, even if the activity was training a crow to do tricks. She only wished she could stop the girl from making up stories. They got more and more bizarre every time. There seemed to be no way to stop Christina from imagining such things. She sat at the kitchen table. It had begun to rain. She knew Christina must come home soon if she were to avoid getting soaked.

The kitchen door flew open.

"Mama! Mama! Wait till you hear what I did today! I learned a new trick! There was this boy—out on the old grass road on the way from school—wait till you hear how I scared him! It was just starting to rain, and there was lightning—pretty blue lightning—and this boy was walking toward me...."

Author Spotlight: Bob MacKenzie

Canadian poet, performer, and arts reviewer Bob MacKenzie has been writing poetry, prose fiction, arts criticism, and songs since 1965. Reflection, his first book of poetry, was published in 1965.

He has published poetry in hundreds of newspapers, magazines, journals and anthologies in Canada, The United States, and worldwide; has, with noted Canadian printmaker G. Brender a Brandis, published five prints of his poems as signed and numbered limited edition prints and The Little Song, a signed and numbered limited edition book; has published/broadcast arts commentary in local, regional, and national Canadian media; and has, with the performance group Poem de Terre, had seven releases of spoken word and songs, including War & Love (2006).

He is the only Canadian poet (one of only two in North America) for whom an art gallery has devoted an entire visual-arts exhibition to his work and possibly the only poet to have artist-versions of his poetry in Canada Council's National Art Bank and has won numerous awards for poetry, prose, and scripts, including a prestigious Ontario Arts Council Grant.

Dark Matter Press
Kingston Ontario
A Canadian Publisher

Author photograph by Annie MacKenzie